Printed in the United States of America
First Edition
1 3 5 7 9 10 8 6 4 2
V475-2873-013152
Library of Congress Control Number: 2013933221
ISBN: 978-1-4231-8408-9
For more Disney Press fun, visit www.disneybooks.com
For more Buddies fun, visit www.disney.com/buddies

SUSTAINABLE
FORESTRY
INITIATIVE

Certified Chain of Custody
Promoting Sustainable Forestry

www.sfiprogram.org
SFI-01054

The SFI label applies to the text stock

Adapted by Tracey West

Based on the character "Air Bud," created by Kevin DiCicco

Based on characters created by Robert Vince & Anna McRoberts

Super Buddies is based on the screenplay written by Robert Vince and Anna McRoberts

DISNEP PRESS

New York

CHAPTER 1

The morning sun rose on Fernfield Farms, streaming into the window in Bartleby's bedroom. Budderball, a big puppy with golden shaggy fur, stirred in his sleep. A delicious smell hit his nose.

Breakfast!

Excited, Budderball jumped up. Today was a special day. It was

1

Bartleby's birthday, which meant there would be a party. And hamburgers. And hot dogs. And cake. And . . . Budderball couldn't wait any longer. He jumped up and licked Bartleby's face.

"Good morning," Bartleby said, giggling.

With Budderball urging him, Bartleby quickly got dressed and then put a red football jersey on the puppy. They hurried down the farmhouse stairs to the kitchen, where Grandpa Marvin, a big man with a white beard, was cooking breakfast.

"Happy birthday, Bartleby. Your birthday breakfast is almost ready," he said.

"Thanks, Gramps!" Bartleby said, sitting down at the table.

Budderball barked and put his paws on Bartleby's legs. He was so hungry!

"Don't worry, I got you covered, boy," Bartleby said, patting the puppy's head. He walked over to the bag of dog food on the counter. The bag had a picture of a dog wearing a super hero cape on the front. It also had a message on the front in bright letters: "Collect all 5 Rings of Inspiron for your own Captain Canine to wear."

Budderball wagged his tail. Captain Canine was the best super hero ever!

Bartleby reached into the bag. "Do you think today might be our lucky day?"

He poured the chow into Budderball's large food dish, and an orange plastic ring as wide as a cereal bowl slid out.

"No way! The last Ring of Inspiron!" Bartleby cried. "Now I have the whole set!"

Budderball happily dug into his food. The rings were from his and Bartleby's favorite comic book, and they had been collecting them for months. It was so cool to have a complete set.

At the table, Bartleby began to draw a comic book frame on a piece of paper. Gramps placed a plate heaped with pancakes, eggs, and bacon in front of him.

"Come on, eat up!" Gramps urged.

"It's your birthday and you need your strength for all the fun you, me, and Budderball are going to have today."

Then Gramps pulled a wrapped present from behind his back.

"For me?" Bartleby asked, unwrapping it. Then he gasped. "It's issue number one! The first-ever *Kid Courageous and Captain Canine*! I can't believe it. How did you ever find it?"

Gramps looked at Bartleby with a sparkle in his eye.

"I have my ways," Gramps said. "Now don't let your birthday breakfast get cold!"

Budderball barked in agreement. Breakfast was the most important meal of the day . . . next to lunch, and dinner, and snack time, and . . .

"By the way, have either of you seen my dentures?" Gramps asked. "I had to put in my spare this morning."

But Bartleby and Budderball hadn't seen them. Gramps left to do his chores on the farm, and Budderball jumped on the seat next to Bartleby. He put his paw on the comic book, excited. He and Bartleby had always wanted to read the first issue of *Kid Courageous and Captain Canine*.

"All right, Budderball," Bartleby said turning the page. "I'll read it out loud."

Then he began to read.

Earth Year: 1985

*F*ar, far away, in a whole other galaxy, is the planet Inspiron. The Inspirons lived in peace for thousands of years, protected by the five power rings: pink, blue, silver, orange, and green.

But all that changed when the

Darkonians, led by the evil Commander Drex, arrived seeking to capture the rings and use the rings' power for evil.

Princess Jorala of the Inspirons gave the power rings to Captain Megasis, the most trusted member of the Inspiron people. Megasis headed to Earth in his spaceship, but Drex followed him. Beams of energy from the Darkonian ship blasted the Inspiron craft.

Captain Megasis knew that he couldn't escape—but he had a plan. He shot a torpedo at Drex's ship. Then he shot the rings out of the ship in a torpedo headed toward Earth. Next Megasis exploded his own ship. Drex thought he had destroyed himself and the rings.

But Captain Megasis had escaped in a space pod. He crash-landed in Seattle, Washington. To avoid capture, he transformed into the first life-form he saw: a shaggy brown-and-white dog.

He befriended a young boy, Jack Schaeffer. Jack's father had been a police officer. Jack wanted to fight crime to honor his father's memory. Megasis wanted to search for the lost rings and help his new friend.

The two became super heroes: Kid Courageous and Captain Canine. Jack created a comic book and told the stories of their adventures. Together, they helped right many wrongs . . . but they never found the rings.

CHAPTER 3

Budderball barked happily. The part of the comic when Captain Megasis turned into a dog was his favorite.

"Captain Canine is still waiting for the rings to be activated, and he and Kid Courageous, who's a grown-up now, are still fighting crime in the meantime," Bartleby said. "But he has never given up hope . . . he will find the rings one day."

Budderball shrugged. He had no idea where they were.

Both Budderball and Bartleby would have been surprised to learn what had really happened to the rings. When the torpedo carrying the rings hit Earth all those years before, it slammed into a barn in Fernfield—Gramps's barn!

Gramps never knew what had hit his barn. The torpedo disintegrated as soon as it hit. And the rings sank deep into the dirt of the barn floor.

But that was long ago—so long that Gramps never even thought about the crash much anymore. And today he was busy planning Bartleby's birthday party.

A police siren sounded outside the farmhouse, and Bartleby dropped the comic and got up to look out the window. Sheriff Dan's brown police cruiser pulled up out front, red lights flashing. The car stopped and Sheriff Dan got out with Deputy Sniffer, his loyal bloodhound. Budderball thought that Sniffer was a great deputy. He took his job very seriously.

Budderball and Bartleby ran outside, and they stopped, surprised. Blue and yellow balloons decorated the fence around the farmhouse. Sheriff Dan waved, and then all of Bartleby's friends and their Buddies jumped out from behind tractors and haystacks. His friends held a banner that read HAPPY BIRTHDAY, SUPER BARTLEBY!

"Surprise! Happy birthday!" they yelled.

Budderball ran to greet the Buddies— his three brothers, B-Dawg, Buddha, and Mudbud, and one sister, Rosebud. Each golden retriever puppy wore a hero costume to match his or her kid.

Suddenly, the sound of super hero music blared throughout the farm. The door to the hayloft on the top floor of the barn opened. There stood Gramps, in his own hero costume. His cape was a checkered tablecloth, his boots were black rubber farm boots, and he had a leather tool belt around his waist and welding goggles on his face. A big blue "G" decorated his shirt.

"The amazing Grandpa-Man is here!" he announced. Then, to everyone's amazement, he flew down from the barn on a zip line and crashed into a haystack!

"Dude, that was major sweet," said Bartleby's friend Pete.

Gramps climbed out of the haystack and struck his best hero pose. Then he pulled an enormous gift-wrapped box from behind the hay bales.

"Surprise!" Gramps yelled.

Bartleby couldn't believe it. "Wait, another gift?"

"You only turn twelve once, kiddo," Gramps said with a wink.

Budderball ran over to see what was in the box. Bartleby pulled out two perfectly made super hero costumes— and one was exactly Budderball's size.

"Wow, Grandpa-Man! You rock!" Bartleby said, hugging Gramps.

Bartleby and Budderball changed behind a hay bale. They emerged wearing matching costumes: blue suits with gold trim and blue capes.

Gramps clapped his hands. "Now it's time for the Super Bartleby birthday treasure hunt!" he announced as he handed out lists and maps of the farm to all the kids.

"Now, split up into teams of two," Gramps instructed. "When you hear the bugle, the hunt begins! The first team to find all the treasures on the list gets a Grandpa-Man super hero prize. So have at it!"

Gramps pulled up a bugle attached to his utility belt and blew into it. Sam and his sister, Alice, teamed up quickly, and so did Pete and Bartleby. Billy was left by himself, but Gramps quickly dashed over and put his arm around him.

"Looks like you're with me, kiddo," Gramps said. "Let's have at it!"

Alice read from the list. "'Number one, a circular object.' Uhhh . . . I have an idea. Come on!"

The kids and Gramps raced off. Sheriff Dan decided to do some fishing, leaving the Buddies alone.

"Come on, boys, treasure time!" Rosebud said eagerly. "I love searching for treasure. You heard Alice. Let's help! We need to find a circular object."

"My basketball is a circular treasure, yo, but it's at home," B-Dawg remarked.

The Buddies raced off in different directions, excited to find the treasure.

CHAPTER 4

B-Dawg and Rosebud headed for the chicken coop.

"An egg is a circular object," Rosebud said. "Go get one, B-Dawg!"

"Uh, I don't know, Sis," he replied nervously.

"Come on, it's just a few chickens in there . . . and one out here," she teased.

"I'm not a chicken," B-Dawg insisted. "I would go in, but, you know, I just don't want to get the chicken pox."

Rosebud shook her head. "You don't get chicken pox from chickens, B-Dawg. If you're too scared, I'll go."

"This dawg's not afraid of nothing, let alone scrawny chickens," B-Dawg insisted.

He reluctantly walked into the chicken coop. The chickens inside began to cluck and flap their wings.

"Yo, alpha dog in the house," he said boldly.

He made a dash for the nearest nest and gently put an egg in his mouth. Then he looked up—and froze. Betty, the biggest chicken he'd ever seen, stared at him with her black eyes.

"Don't even think about it," she squawked.

B-Dawg nervously put down the egg.

"I think I'd better teach this young'n a lesson," Betty clucked.

Seconds later, B-Dawg ran out of the coop, covered in feathers.

"Run, dawgs! Giant chicken in the house! I am flying the coop!" he yelled.

Over at the bull pen, Budderball was talking to Mr. Bull. He was hoping to get the big bull's nose ring for the treasure hunt. But Mr. Bull just roared loudly, and Budderball ran away.

I wish I could be big and strong like Mr. Bull, he thought. But I'm just a puppy!

Rosebud went to the pony paddock, where she found two young Shetland ponies, Strawberry and Lollipop. Strawberry had pink ribbons braided into her mane and tail, and Lollipop had purple ribbons. Rosebud was hoping to borrow one of their circular horseshoes for the treasure hunt.

"I wish I could give you one, but these things are stuck to me like a bad habit," Lollipop explained.

Mudbud went to the pigpen, where he found Big Mama, her three piglets, and Curly, a large teenage pig. The pen was sparkling clean, and the pigs looked miserable.

"Whoa, whoa, dude and dudettes. Where's all the mud?" Mudbud asked.

Curly tried to explain, talking in pig Latin. "Armer-fay Arvin-may crubbed-say s-uay lean-cay or-fay ee-thay arty-pay, Udbud-may," he said, and then he translated. "Farmer Marvin scrubbed us clean for the party, Mudbud."

Mudbud hated to see his pig friends so bummed out. He turned on a hose, and soon the pen was filled with mud. The pigs cheered and started rolling around in the mud, and Mudbud joined them.

"Woohoo! I am as happy as a pig in

mud!" Mudbud cheered. "Any chance you guys know of any circular objects?"

"Ere's-thay lways-aay y-may ail-tay? Ut-bay ou'd-yay ave-hay oo-tay ake-tay ee-may ith-way ou-yay, ude-day!" Curly said in pig Latin. "There's always my tail, but you'd have to take me with you, dude."

"Uh, I'll think of something a little more portable," Mudbud said. "Catch you dude and dudettes on the flip side!"

Buddha had decided to visit the cow pasture. He sat in peaceful meditation.

"I'd love to stay with you enlightened beings, but I must procure something round, much like your bell," Buddha said to the cows. "May I borrow it?"

"If you take our bell Farmer Marvin might lose us when we wander off to graze," one of the cows said.

Buddha nodded. "That would not be good. My search continues, then. *Namaste*."

Buddha ran off to join the other Buddies. They met outside the barn. Mudbud was covered in mud.

"Well, other than Mudbud's new coat, looks like we're all empty-pawed," Rosebud remarked.

B-Dawg nodded toward the barn. "Maybe there's treasure inside there? So far the only treasure I've found is myself."

"The treasure you speak of, B-Dawg,

is not real but a metaphoric treasure," Buddha informed him.

Budderball shook his head. "I don't even know what you just said."

The Buddies followed B-Dawg inside the dusty barn. Cows stood in their stalls, peacefully munching on hay. The Buddies sniffed the ground, searching for a circular object for the treasure hunt.

"The only circular object I want to find is a doughnut, and I certainly don't see one of those in here!" Budderball said.

He was sniffing alongside a stall when he suddenly spotted a dim light coming up from one of the boards. Curious, he pushed the loose board aside and saw something poking out of the dirt.

"Look, Buddies!" he called to his friends. "In there! Something shiny and round!"

The Buddies raced over.

"Let the dirt maestro do the deed," Mudbud offered.

He quickly dug through the dirt under the boards, unearthing five rings, each one a different color: blue, orange, silver, green, and pink. He nudged one with his muzzle and it began to glow. Then all five rings magically floated in the air!

"Whoa. Those look just like the Rings of Inspiron," Budderball said.

"From the comic book?" Rosebud asked.

"Exactly!" Budderball exclaimed. "They come in my puppy food. Gramps must be collecting them, too."

"Dude, why'd he just leave them in a pile of dirt?" Mudbud asked.

"Maybe Gramps buried them, and that's what we're supposed to find on this treasure hunt," Budderball guessed. "Bartleby will be so excited to see another full set. Grab one!"

"I want pink!" Rosebud cried.

"I want bling!" said B-Dawg.

"Bling is not a color, B-Dawg," Buddha pointed out.

"You are right about that, dawg,"

B-Dawg agreed. "Bling is a state of mind."

He slid his head through the silver ring and it shrunk perfectly to fit around his neck. The rest of the Buddies did the same. Buddha wore the orange ring, Rosebud wore the pink ring, Mudbud wore the green, and Budderball wore the blue.

Before they could discuss what had just happened, a bugle blew outside.

"Oh, sweet mama! It's the birthday cake bugle!" Budderball said. Then he raced out of the barn.

Mudbud was impressed. "That dude can move for food."

The other Buddies followed him

outside. Budderball trotted up to a huge super hero birthday cake with yellow and blue icing. He licked his face in anticipation.

"All this treasure hunting has made me hungry," he said. "Lucky for me it's my sworn duty as man's best friend to taste-test the cake for quality control."

Budderball snuck under the table, getting into the ultimate crumb-eating position. The kids ran up moments later, and Bartleby immediately noticed the Buddies' new collars.

"Hey, the Rings of Inspiron!" Bartleby cried. "Did you guys find them in my backpack?"

He quickly checked his backpack,

but his rings were all there. Bartleby frowned, confused.

"Budderball, have you been collecting them without telling me? Where have you been hiding these filthy things? Budderball?"

He looked around but didn't see his puppy anywhere.

"Where is that little rascal? It's not like him to miss cake," Bartleby said.

Gramps held up the cake slicer. "All right! Who's hungry?"

At that moment Budderball popped out from under the table.

"Ta-daaaaaaaa!"

He had Gramps's missing dentures in his mouth! Everyone laughed at how silly he looked with a mouthful of big white teeth.

"Oh, Budderball, you found my teeth! I've been looking all over for them," Gramps said. "Thanks, big fella!"

And then it was time for cake, games, and puppy treats. Alice and Sam had found the most objects and were crowned winners of the treasure hunt. The Buddies had so much fun that they didn't think about how strange it was to find five glowing rings in the barn.

They didn't know it, but they had found the *real* Rings of Inspiron!

CHAPTER 5

Before the end of the party, Bartleby gathered his friends and showed them the first issue of *Kid Courageous and Captain Canine.*

"The rumor in the comic book world is that Captain Canine and Jack are actually real," Bartleby informed them after he explained the story.

"Dude, have they found the rings yet?" Pete asked.

"Not yet," Bartleby said. "Megasis—I mean, Captain Canine—is still waiting for them to be activated. He and Kid Courageous, who's a grown-up now, are fighting crime in the meantime. But Megasis has never given up hope. He will find the rings one day, I just know it."

Budderball wagged his tail. He knew it, too. Captain Canine was the greatest super hero ever!

After a long day of birthday games, Budderball fell fast asleep that night. The next morning, he woke up as hungry as ever.

He looked up at the bed. Bartleby was still sound asleep. No problem. Budderball knew what to do. He quietly sneaked into the kitchen.

"Morning snack, here I come!" he whispered.

As usual, a towel was hanging from the refrigerator door handle. Just a little tug and the door would open.

Budderball didn't notice, but at that moment, the blue ring around his neck began to glow. Budderball gripped the towel in his mouth and pulled.

Crash! The whole door fell right off!

"Sweet mama, that was awesome!" Budderball exclaimed.

He dove in and started gnawing on some salami.

Over at Billy's house, Billy and B-Dawg were shooting hoops in their pajamas. Then Billy ran off to take out the garbage for his mom.

B-Dawg grabbed the ball in his paws. He leapt up to make a jump shot, and his silver collar started to glow. His whole body began to stretch like a rubber band until he reached all the way to the net! He dunked the ball right into the hoop.

"Oh, baby, slam dunk!" he yelled.

Meanwhile, Buddha and his kid, Sam, were at the yoga studio downtown for Buddha's favorite class—morning meditation. Buddha sat back and closed his eyes, chanting.

As he chanted, his orange collar began to glow. His whole body rose from the mat and he began to float in midair! Everyone in the studio had their eyes closed, so nobody saw him.

Buddha opened one eye—and realized that he was floating! Losing concentration, he crashed to the ground.

"That was transcendental," Buddha remarked.

In Pete's backyard, Mudbud was sound asleep on a pile of dirt. Pete called to him from the house.

"Mudbud, bath time! Mom says

she can smell you from the kitchen."

Mudbud's ears perked up.

"Has it been a month already?" he wondered.

Pete came out of the house to look for him, and Mudbud started to panic.

"Oh, no, I'm cornered. Must . . . hide," he said.

As he searched for a hiding place, his green collar began to glow. Then he completely vanished! Pete walked right past him without seeing him.

"Wait a moment, you can't see me?" Mudbud realized. "This is epic! I will never have to bathe again!"

But then the automatic lawn sprinklers came on, and the water drenched Mudbud. He was no longer invisible.

"Sorry, dude, but Mom will want me to add soap to that water," Pete said as Mudbud whined.

Meanwhile, in Fernfield Park, Rosebud watched Alice play a soccer game. Just as Alice was about to shoot a goal, one of the members of the opposing team tackled her. The ref didn't see it, and some of the players on the sidelines were laughing.

The ball was still in play, and Rosebud couldn't resist. She raced onto the field, and her pink collar began to glow.

Zoooooom! Rosebud charged at super speed, becoming a pink blur on the field. The ball soared past the stunned goalie into the net.

Nobody knew what had happened. The ref gave the goal to Alice, and her team cheered.

"Now that's girl power!" Rosebud remarked.

By now, all the Buddies knew that something strange was going on. They agreed to meet at Town Hall. Budderball ran up and saw Buddha and B-Dawg waiting for him.

"Something strange is happening to me!" Budderball cried. "I am strong like a bull, just like I've always wanted to be!"

"Where are Mudbud and Rosebud?" Buddha asked.

A voice answered him. "What do you mean? I'm right here."

The voice seemed to be coming from a bush—with puppy eyes!

"Aaaah!" B-Dawg cried. "Dawg, you are less Mudbud and more Shrub-Bud."

Mudbud's camouflage faded away, and now his siblings could see him.

"It keeps happening to me," Mudbud explained. "Here one minute, gone the next."

"We are just missing Rosebud, then," Buddha said. "Fashionably late as usual."

Then Rosebud appeared in a blur, speaking really fast.

"Nope, right on time," she said. "It's

like I'm so fast that everything is last season by the time it gets to me."

"The dudette's got speed!" Mudbud said, impressed.

Budderball turned to Buddha. "Anything out of the ordinary going on with you?"

"I'm finding myself to have excellent mind control, more than I ever imagined that I could," Buddha reported. "I'm able to move things with my mind, including myself. It's safe to conclude these rings have done something extraordinary to us ordinary pups," Buddha said. "Our natural gifts have been heightened."

"But how?" Budderball asked.

"Just think of the good we can do," Buddha said. "We can protect humans from those with bad Karma."

"Dudes, that's what we love to do anyways," Mudbud pointed out. "Now we can do it in an epic way."

"You're all right!" Rosebud agreed. "I love making Fernfield a better place to live. I say we give it a shot. Girl power!"

Budderball was excited. "This is like a dream come true," he said. "I'm all for the super hero gig, but we're going to need our super hero suits. In fact it's one of the rules of being a super hero: a super hero must always conceal their true identity to protect the ones they love. Suit up and meet me back here later. Who's in?"

Budderball held out his paw, and each of the other Buddies put a paw on top of his.

"And . . . break!" they yelled.

The Five Rings of Inspiron had been activated, but the Buddies weren't the only ones to figure that out.

In Seattle, Jack Schaeffer and Captain Canine got a signal from the rings, coming from somewhere in Fernfield.

And deep in outer space, Commander Drex got the signal, too. He and his henchman, Monk-E, steered their ship for a new course: Earth. . . .

CHAPTER 6

Later that day, the five Buddies strolled down Main Street in their hero costumes.

Budderball let out a cheer. "Fernfield, no more fear, the Super Buddies are . . . going to kick butt?" he tried.

"Dawg, that was not very poetic," B-Dawg said.

"I was trying to rhyme something with 'fear,'" Budderball said.

"Uhhh, how about 'here'?" Rosebud suggested.

"Rosebud, you're a serious genius!" Budderball cried. "Fernfield, no more fear, the Super Buddies are here!"

"All we need is someone to help," Rosebud said, and then they heard a cry.

"Help! Someone help! I'm stuck!"

The Buddies raced around the corner—and found a little gray cat stuck in a tree.

"I think I know what to do," Budderball said.

He charged at the tree like an angry

bull. His collar glowed blue and his body grew so that he was big and strong.

Bam! He slammed into the tree just as Sheriff Dan and Sniffer showed up in their police cruiser. The tree shook, and the cat jumped out of it.

"Thank you!" she mewed, and then ran off.

Crack! Budderball had hit the tree so hard that it fell over, crushing the police car! Luckily, Sheriff Dan and Deputy Sniffer were okay.

"Oops!" Budderball said. "Beginner's error."

"We just need to practice a little more, that's all," Mudbud said.

The Super Buddies raced off, looking for someone else to help. They patrolled the streets until it became dark. Budderball was thinking about going home and getting a snack when he saw movement in the Fernfield Candy Store. He stopped.

"Guys, the candy store is open. Maybe we can go in," he said.

"It's not open, Budderball," Rosebud said.

"Yes, it is. Look!" Budderball insisted.

He looked in the window again—and gasped. Two thieves dressed in black were stuffing candy and money into bags. Poor Mr. Swanson, the owner of the shop, was tied to a chair!

"A job for the Super Buddies!" B-Dawg said. "Let's roll!"

The Buddies raced inside.

Rosebud acted first. She tied up the first thief with red rope licorice. Then Budderball loaded his mouth with gumballs and shot them rapid-fire at the other thief, knocking her down. She got up and quickly freed her friend, and he ran for the door. To stop him, Mudbud turned invisible and gave the thief a wedgie by pulling hard on the elastic of his pants. The elastic snapped, sending the thief crashing into the wall.

The woman tried to run next, but B-Dawg stretched across the opening.

She bounced off him and landed on top of the other thief with a crash. To finish them off, Buddha used his mind to lift a big vat of caramel. Then he dumped the sticky goo on the thieves, trapping them.

"Where did those super puppies come from?" Mr. Swanson wondered.

Sheriff Dan and Sniffer arrived. They went inside the store to take care of the thieves just as a news van pulled up.

"If I hadn't seen it with my own eyes, I would never believe it," Mr. Swanson told the reporter. "I was saved by super puppies!"

The reporter turned to the camera. "Well, there you have it, folks. It seems a group of 'super puppies' have saved the day! Who are these pup crusaders? Stay tuned for the latest developments on this incredible story. This is Sofia Ramirez reporting live from the Fernfield Candy Store, signing off."

CHAPTER 7

After a big day of being super heroes, the Buddies went home to get some sleep. But in the morning they headed out early, eager to save the day again.

They didn't know it, but Commander Drex had followed the signal of the power rings right to the pigpen on Gramps's farm.

Monk-E looked out the pod's window. "How exciting to explore a planet in another universe, Commander!" Drex's henchman looked like a monkey with pale green fur. He wore a silver space suit.

"Maybe so, but you'll never have that pleasure," Drex said. "You need to stay right here with our ship to operate mission control."

"Okay, Commander. Some other time, then? Good luck out there!" Monk-E said with a salute.

Drex opened the hatch and stepped out into the pigpen. Taller than a human, he had green skin and three long fingers on each hand. His bald head was huge, and he had large black eyes. His uniform was made of sparkly gray material.

He marched up to Curly, the teenage pig. Then he pressed a button on the small computer he wore on his wrist. Monk-E's face appeared on the screen.

"Monk-E. I want you to Body Snatch this vile human," Drex snapped.

"Copy that," Monk-E said, typing on the keyboard in front of him. "Uhhh, Commander, according to my research, that is not a hu—"

"Silence, Monk-E!" Drex commanded impatiently. "Initiate Body Snatch now."

"As you wish, Commander," Monk-E said with a shrug.

Drex's eyes glowed green. His wrist computer beeped. Lightning bolts crackled from his body, and then he disappeared. He took over Curly's body! The pink pig's skin now glowed with a greenish tint.

Gramps walked up, holding a bucket of slop. "Hello, little piggies, and good morning to ya!" he said cheerfully.

He tossed the bucket of slop into the pen, covering Drex with the goop. Then he spotted the space pod sticking out of the mud and froze.

"I am Commander Drex, feared leader of the Darkonian race," Drex said in a superior tone. "You are to forfeit this planet and the Five Power—"

Gramps screamed and ran toward the safety of the barn before Drex could finish.

Drex, still in pig form, laughed. "Conquering this planet is going to be easier than I thought, and I already thought it was going to be easy." Then he spoke into his wrist computer. "Monk-E, make the pod disappear."

The pod turned invisible, and Drex marched out of the pen to look for the Rings of Inspiron. He approached Gramps's pickup truck and snorted.

"I'm not surprised that Earthlings use such horrendous ground ships," he said, climbing into the driver's seat. He raised his hooves and electricity shot out of them, starting the ignition. The engine came to life as he contacted Monk-E on his wrist computer.

"Monk-E? What is the location of the rings?" Drex asked.

"Our landing destination was a success," Monk-E reported. "The rings are close by. You should head in the direction of forty-seventh quadrant for 5.2 plions. Copy?"

"Copy," Drex replied. "The sooner I can get out of this disgusting Earth creature, the better."

The truck pulled out of the farm with a squeal.

CHAPTER 8

Gramps called Sheriff Dan and Sniffer to tell them about the UFO, but when they got to the farm, they didn't see it. Monk-E had cloaked the pod, just as Drex had ordered, making it invisible.

"Hey, Sheriff!" Pete called out as the kids rode their bikes up to the farm.

"Is everything okay?" Bartleby asked.

"Just a little misunderstanding," Sheriff Dan explained, pushing his hat back on his head. "Your grandpa thought he saw a . . . um . . . UFO in the pigpen."

Alice's blue eyes got wide. "UFO? Like a spaceship?" she asked.

"The sun is awfully hot. Probably just a mild case of heatstroke," Sheriff Dan guessed.

Bartleby turned to his friends. "Well, I know an awful lot about aliens. Let's go investigate."

Sheriff Dan and Sniffer drove off in the busted cruiser, and the kids approached the pigpen, curious.

Alice made a face. "Just a bunch of

muddy pigs. And 'mud pies.' Gross."

Bartleby climbed over the green metal fence and landed inside the pen. He slowly stepped through the muck, searching for evidence. Suddenly, he bumped into something. But there was nothing there!

"Wait, what was that?" he asked.

Bartleby touched the space in front of him, and he could feel something. But whatever he was touching was invisible.

"It's like metal," Bartleby said. "I think there's some kind of button."

He pressed the button, and the cloaking field dropped. Drex's space pod appeared in front of him.

Bartleby's mouth dropped open. "Whoa."

"Epic," Pete agreed.

Inside the pod, Monk-E panicked. He pounded on all the buttons on the console, trying to reach Drex.

"Commander! Mayday! Mayday! Earthlings moving in!" he shouted.

But Drex was having a hard time, too. He had steered the truck to Main Street—and then crashed into a fence pole. A crowd of people had gathered to marvel at the green pig driving the truck.

Monk-E's face popped up on Drex's wrist computer.

"We have intruders!" Monk-E cried.

The Buddies are dressed as super heroes
for Bartleby's birthday party on Bartleby's
grandpa's farm.

The Buddies discover five magical rings
that give them super powers!

B-Dawg and Rosebud explore the chicken coop.

The biggest chicken on the farm is B-Dawg!

The Buddies attend Bartleby's birthday
party in style!

Budderball's ring glows blue. He's one strong pup!

Does somebody need saving?
The Super Buddies are here to help!

It is up to the Super Buddies to help
the cat down from the tree.

Rosebud ties up a thief in the candy store
with a red licorice rope!

Pups to the rescue! Justice never tasted so sweet.

Deputy Sniffer arrives at the scene of the candy store crime in his pajamas!

Needing a disguise when he arrives on Earth, the evil Commander Drex body-snatches Curly the pig.

The Buddies' idol, Captain Megasis, soars
through smoke to save a little girl.

Captain Megasis joins forces with the Super
Buddies to teach them how to use their powers
in the name of good.

Monk-E wants to be an eggs-pert in being
a good earthling.

The pups are super with or without magical
rings—because you don't need super
powers to be a super hero.

"I've got my own problems. Deal with it!" Drex growled. "But whatever you do, keep all Earthlings away from your pod."

While Drex and Monk-E spoke, Bartleby examined the pod. He noticed a symbol that looked like a triangle with two sweeping tails on the bottom.

"That symbol looks familiar. I've seen it somewhere before," Bartleby said.

He touched the symbol, and an electric shock knocked him back into the mud.

Inside the pod, Monk-E felt bad. "I hope that didn't hurt," he said, although he knew the boy couldn't hear him. "Just following orders. Sorry, Earthling."

"Whoa," Bartleby said, climbing to his feet. "What was that?"

"Oh, ick!" Alice said with a grimace. "Are you okay?"

"Yeah," Bartleby replied, wiping himself off. Then the pod disappeared right before his eyes!

"Yo, where'd it go?" Billy asked.

Bartleby looked thoughtful. "Something weird is going on. That symbol . . . Wait, I know! Come on!"

He climbed out of the pigpen, and his friends followed him as he raced across the field.

On Main Street, Sheriff Dan pulled

his cruiser up to the scene of an accident. Two cars had hit each other head-on while avoiding Gramps's truck, which was up against a fence pole.

Sheriff Dan exited the cruiser and pushed through the crowd. He stopped when he saw a pig in the driver's seat of Gramps's smashed-up truck.

"Holy pork chops! Pigs *can* drive!" he exclaimed. "Not well, but they can drive!"

He looked down at his deputy. "Deputy Sniffer, quick! My lasso."

Drex watched, impressed, as the crowd parted to let Sheriff Dan through.

"Aha," he said. "Perhaps he is the true ruler of these people."

Drex climbed out of the truck as Deputy Sniffer brought the lasso to Sheriff Dan.

"Thanks, partner," Sheriff Dan said. "Let's hog-tie this here pig! Giddy up! I've heard of green eggs and ham, but never a green ham. Guess there's always a first."

Sheriff Dan quickly lassoed Drex. The pig's eyes glowed green with anger as Sheriff Dan loaded him into the cruiser.

Drex's eyes narrowed. *Very soon, you will rue the day that you dared to stand against Commander Drex!* he thought.

CHAPTER 9

A few blocks away, the Super Buddies were on hero patrol. They turned a corner and saw smoke rising from a building in the distance.

"Oh, no! This looks like trouble!" Budderball cried.

"Another rescue for the Super Buddies, dudes!" Mudbud cheered.

The Buddies ran to the scene of the fire. They could hear fire engines in the distance, but the firefighters had not arrived yet. Smoke billowed from several windows of the apartment building. A little girl with blond hair was on the top floor, yelling out the window.

"Help! Help me! Help!" she cried.

Budderball knew what had to be done. "Follow me, Super Buddies!"

"Let a girl lead the way," Rosebud said. "Hang on."

She raced off at super speed and came back seconds later.

"She's in 8B, but the door's locked," Rosebud reported.

The Buddies followed her into the building and up to the eighth floor. Budderball used his super strength to crash right through the door, taking it off its hinges.

"Doors aren't an issue for Super Budderball!" he cheered.

Rosebud coughed. "I can't see anything through this smoke!"

Buddha closed his eyes. "Smoke, disperse," he said calmly.

Buddha concentrated, and the smoke cleared. They could see the little girl crouched in a corner, scared. Mudbud raced over and tugged on the girl's pant leg, urging her to walk toward the door.

"Follow us, yo!" B-Dawg shouted, but the girl was too scared to move.

Then . . . *crash!* The ceiling caved in, blocking the path to the door. Buddha concentrated on the wreckage as hard as he could, but it barely moved.

"I can't move it!" he cried.

"What do we do now, super dudes?" Mudbud asked.

"We're super heroes," Budderball reminded them. "Let's not panic."

"I think that train already left the station, dawgs," B-Dawg pointed out.

Things looked grim. But just as they were about to give up hope, a shadowy figure in a super hero costume jumped over the burning debris. The dogs watched as the hero appeared through the smoke. It was Captain Canine! He raced over to the girl.

"Quickly, come with me!" he said.

The girl grabbed hold of Captain Canine's collar and he led her through the burning debris to safety. The Buddies quickly followed.

Outside, the puppies and Captain Canine stayed to the side as the girl ran into the arms of her mom. The firefighters had arrived and were aiming their hoses at the blaze.

"Dudes, that was too close for comfort," Budderball said with a shudder. Then he turned to his hero. "Captain Canine? You're really real? I mean, I already believed you were."

Captain Canine looked at the Buddies. "You five puppies have the Rings of Inspiron? You have no idea how long I've been searching for those."

"You mean we have the real rings?" Budderball asked.

"And we're really in the presence of a real super hero . . . and an alien?" asked Buddha.

Captain Canine nodded. "Yes, that's true. I am Captain Canine from the planet Inspiron."

Excited, Budderball jumped up and down. "Bartleby is not going to believe this! The whole thing is true!"

"You five have been pretty busy,"

Captain Canine said. "I've been tracking you since the rings were first activated. We haven't got much time."

They started to leave, but Rosebud spoke up. "Guys, where is B-Dawg?"

They turned and saw B-Dawg walking toward the crowd in front of the apartment building.

"This isn't good," Captain Canine said.

The crowd had gathered around the girl and her family, and the reporter was there with her cameraman. B-Dawg walked right toward them.

"The Super Pups and Captain Canine saved me!" the girl told the reporter. "There, look!"

The reporter got right on it. "Sofia

Ramirez reporting to you live with the real Super Pups," she said. "Here is one of them now—and there are more puppies behind him!"

Rosebud ran up to him. "We can't be on camera, B-Dawg. Let's hightail it out of here!"

The Buddies all raced back to the alley, where Captain Canine was waiting for them.

"What did you pups think you were doing back there?" he asked sternly. "You've completely revealed yourselves to Drex and put your families in danger."

"Why are you trippin', Captain Canine? Everyone loves us," B-Dawg said.

"Drex is very dangerous," Captain Canine said in a serious tone.

The Buddies stared at him, alarmed.

"Can't you stop him?" Rosebud asked.

"I am merely a dog. I have no superpowers. Only the holder of those rings can stop him now. Where did you find them?" Captain Canine asked.

"At my grandpa's farm," Budderball replied.

"Drex will definitely go there. We must hurry," Captain Canine said.

Then the six super heroes raced toward Fernfield Farms.

CHAPTER 10

Back at the farm, Monk-E had decided to ignore his orders from Commander Drex. He left the pod, eager to explore Earth. The first creatures he came across were the ponies, Lollipop and Strawberry, and they were happy to talk to him.

"So your human commander,

Farmer Marvin, takes care of you, grooms you, and feeds you carrots, but doesn't require you to do any work?" Monk-E asked after the ponies told him about life on the farm.

"Well, he does take us for the occasional ride," Strawberry reported.

"And we go to shows at the county fair," Lollipop added.

Monk-E was very impressed. That sounded like a good deal!

The kids, meanwhile, were inside the farmhouse kitchen, frantically flipping through comic books.

Then the TV caught their attention. The words on the screen read SUPER PUPS SAVE THE DAY AGAIN?

"Rumor is that these five super puppies are related to Captain Canine," said Sofia Ramirez, the reporter.

"*Five* super puppies?" Billy asked.

"Mudbud *has* been disappearing a lot lately," Pete realized.

"Buddha has been acting rather strange at his morning meditation," Sam added.

"Budderball only ate once today, and that is NOT normal," Bartleby informed them.

"You know, come to think of it, Rosebud has been wearing the same outfit two days in a row!" Alice said.

The friends all looked at each other.

"Our Buddies are super heroes!" Billy said.

"The Super Pups? But how?" Bartleby wondered.

On the screen, the little girl was talking about her amazing rescue. "They had rings like the ones that come in the bags of puppy food, but theirs were glowing," she said.

Bartleby jumped up. "Those rings! The Buddies have the REAL Rings of Inspiron. And that symbol means that the evil Drex might be here in Fernfield. The Buddies could be in trouble!"

"I think we're *all* in trouble, dudes!" Pete pointed out.

"We'd better tell Sheriff Dan," Alice said.

The friends raced back to their bikes. As they hurried to the sheriff's office, Sheriff Dan was taking a nap at his desk. Inside the cell, Drex wiggled out of the ropes. His eyes glowed green, and electricity shot from his hooves.

Seconds later, he was inside Sheriff Dan's body—and poor Sheriff Dan was inside Curly the pig's body!

The kids rushed in just as Drex, in his new body, walked toward the door.

"Sheriff Dan, are we ever glad to see you," Pete said breathlessly.

"The spaceship is real," Bartleby said. "It belongs to the evil Drex, who came to Earth to capture the Rings of Inspiron, which we are pretty sure our Buddies have!"

Sheriff Dan listened with an odd, blank look on his face. Alice eyed him suspiciously. His skin looked faintly green. Then he spoke, and his voice didn't sound like Sheriff Dan's at all—it was Drex's deep, evil voice.

"Aren't you a genius! I am Commander Drex, feared leader of the Darkonian race. Hand over the puppies now or prepare for your doom!" he demanded.

"Uh, guys . . . I don't think that's Sheriff Dan," Alice said.

CHAPTER 11

The Buddies and Captain Canine got to the farm right after the kids left.

"The Rings of Inspiron are the most powerful items in the universe," Captain Canine explained to the puppies. "It's time I showed you just how powerful they really are."

"They seem to work in a mystical

way," Buddha remarked.

"There actually is a logic to it," Captain Canine said. "We all have a vibrational field that none of us can see, but all of us can feel. The rings take your natural skills and abilities and amplify them many times."

Then Captain Canine showed the Buddies how to improve their powers. He took B-Dawg and Mudbud to the chicken coop.

"If you have the skill to elude capture, the rings will allow you to blend into your environment and move through objects, or objects to move through you," he said.

Betty and the other chickens charged

at B-Dawg and Mudbud. Mudbud turned invisible, leaving B-Dawg behind. But at the last second, B-Dawg went invisible, too, and Betty ran right through him!

"Yo, what just happened?" B-Dawg asked when both pups were visible again.

Captain Canine turned to Mudbud. "Camouflage not only saves you, Mudbud. When you focus on another, your invisibility extends to them."

Then they went to the barn, where Captain Canine tested Rosebud's speed with a tennis ball machine.

"If you are quick of foot and mind, you will become supersonic," he told her.

He pushed a button on the machine, and the balls flew out. Rosebud dodged them, but Captain Canine turned up the speed. Rosebud couldn't keep up and got hit by one of the balls.

"Don't limit yourself to moving from point A to point B, Rosebud," he said. "Your speed is capable of so much more, and so are you. Ready?"

Rosebud concentrated very hard, and this time, she ran in a circle, turning into a mini tornado. The tennis balls got sucked inside the whirling wind and fired back at Captain Canine and the other Buddies. They all ducked and ran for cover to get away from the balls.

"Excellent!" Captain Canine cheered.

He trained Budderball inside the bull pen.

"Budderball, you know how to use your strength when in close quarters. But what do you do when you can't reach your opponent?"

"Uh, I use my secret weapon?" Budderball guessed.

Budderball pawed the ground like a bull and snorted. Then he farted and flew through the air like a rocket! He hit a red barrel at the other end of the pen and sent it flying high above the fence.

Captain Canine was impressed. "Well, I'll be. Jet propulsion."

Buddha's training took place in the cow pasture. Buddha concentrated, chanting.

"Now take your powers even further, Buddha," Captain Canine urged him. "Channel your energy by sending out positive vibrations."

Buddha listened. Using his mind, he raised three cows in the air. One began to float up higher, and one floated down, and the third cow spun in circles.

"Better stop," said the spinning cow. "I think I might throw up all four of my stomachs!"

Buddha gently set the three cows back down on the ground.

"Very good, Buddha," Captain Canine told him. "Remember, positive energy will always win over negative energy."

Then they went to the field, where Captain Canine tied a blindfold around B-Dawg's eyes.

"If you are agile, you will become flexible as rubber," Captain Canine advised him.

The Buddies played a game of Marco Polo with their blindfolded friend, calling out "Polo" so he could catch them. B-Dawg ended up twisting his body until he tied himself in a knot!

"I'm cool. This is just my impersonation of a pretzel," B-Dawg said.

"Don't let your ego take control," Captain Canine told him. "Remember, smooth is more important than fast in your case."

"Word. Smooth is fast," B-Dawg said, nodding. "That's totally my new motto, dawg."

B-Dawg untied himself and then stretched out like a starfish, one leg in each direction, so he could tag all four Buddies at once.

"Drex's big weapon is electrical charge," Captain Canine informed them. "B-Dawg, remember that when your ring is activated, your body has the metabolic consistency of rubber. Electricity cannot conduct through rubber. Only you can protect your Buddies from a direct hit."

Then he faced all the Buddies.

"Now that you have mastered your individual skills, it's very important that each of you stop thinking of yourself as an individual," he said. "In order to defeat Drex, you will have to work together, using all your super-powers as one force."

Rosebud nodded. "As a team."

Captain Canine held out a paw, and each of the Buddies put a paw on top of his.

"Together!" they cried.

Drex jumped into the police cruiser and sped down the country roads of

Fernfield with the kids in the backseat. The Buddies and Captain Canine saw the cruiser pull up to the barn.

"Let's go see our kids," Budderball said.

Captain Canine held up a paw. "Wait a second. The Darkonians can possess any life-form and use it as their own. They call it Body Snatch."

He led the Buddies out of sight behind a tractor to watch. Gramps came out of the farmhouse, holding his pitchfork.

"Sheriff, what are you doing back here?" he asked. Then he noticed the kids in the back. "What are the kids doing in your cruiser? Bartleby?"

"Gramps, that's not Sheriff Dan, it's an alien. Watch out!" Bartleby yelled.

Gramps quickly pointed the pitchfork at Drex. The alien just grinned and raised his hands, sending an electric charge at Gramps. *Zap!* Gramps fell to the ground.

"Oh, no!" Budderball cried.

"Don't worry, he's just stunned," Captain Canine assured him.

"Now what, dude?" Mudbud asked.

"We have to be patient," Captain Canine whispered.

Drex ushered the kids to the barn and locked them inside. Satisfied, he stomped over to his space pod and sat at the control panel.

"Where has that cheeky monkey gone?" he mumbled. "Oh, well. Now to make sure that this planet is destroyed after I get those rings."

He pressed some buttons on the panel. Outside, the Buddies and Captain Canine watched as a laser beam projected from the pod all the way out into space.

"Something tells me that ain't good, dawgs," said B-Dawg.

The laser beam extended into space, latched on to a passing meteor, and sent it on a new course—toward Earth!

Gramps woke up and saw the laser beam. He got to his feet and staggered into the farmhouse to get the phone.

"I better call Sheriff Dan," he said, and then he remembered. "Oh, wait . . . that *was* Sheriff Dan."

The TV was on, and an image caught his eye. A news anchorman was talking into the camera.

"Breaking news," the anchorman said. "A meteor has unexpectedly changed course and is heading straight toward Earth! They estimate only hours left before its devastating impact."

Gramps gasped. This whole mess was bigger than a UFO in his pigpen. The whole world was in danger!

CHAPTER 12

Captain Canine knew he had to stop Drex.

"Stay behind the tractor," he told the Buddies. "I will flush out Drex. Remember what I taught you."

He walked out from behind the trailer and approached the pigpen.

"Drex, it's Captain Megasis. Now

show yourself," he demanded.

Drex climbed out of the pod. He recognized the voice of his old foe.

"Megasis!" Drex exclaimed. "But your ship . . . that night? I thought you were dead."

"You thought wrong," Captain Canine told him.

Drex grinned. "After all these years, I look forward to obliterating you once and for all! Without the rings, you have no powers to match me."

"We'll see about that!" Captain Canine growled. He charged at Drex. The villain used his fingers to fire a bolt of green energy at him, but Captain Canine dodged it.

Wham! He hit Drex in the chest, sending him flying back into the mud. Drex sat up and fired another blast at Captain Canine. This one hit, and Captain Canine fell to the ground. The Buddies watched anxiously. The hero looked hurt.

"Captain Canine!" Budderball cried.

Hearing Budderball, Drex turned around. "Now come out wherever you are, you little super poopies," he said with evil glee. "Without your not-so-fearless leader you haven't got a hope. Surrender the Rings of Inspiron and I'll consider sparing your lives."

The Buddies huddled behind the tractor in their hiding place.

"I think it's time to surrender, dawgs," B-Dawg said.

"Captain Canine said that we will have to combine our powers to defeat Drex, remember?" Budderball reminded them.

"It's time to be a team," Rosebud said. "It's time to really be the Super Buddies."

Buddha nodded. "We have to believe in ourselves."

They all put their paws together.

"Super Buddies!" they cried. Then they ran out from behind the tractor.

Budderball stepped up first. "We will never surrender the rings to evil like you, Drex," he said bravely.

Drex walked toward them. "This is going to be like taking a bone from a puppy," he said.

Buddha started to meditate, and the Buddies joined him, creating an energy shield around them. Drex tried to zap them with another green blast, but it bounced right off the shield. It hit Drex, sending him flying.

Angry, Drex got up and fired another charge. This time, B-Dawg stretched his body to cover it.

"Oh, no you didn't. Electricity can't conduct through rubber," B-Dawg said as the blast bounced back at Drex.

Frustrated, Drex aimed his electricity at some tools over by the barn. A pitchfork, a hammer, and a saw all flew toward the Buddies.

"I got this one," Rosebud said confidently.

She quickly ran in circles, moving so fast that she became a mini tornado. Each of the sharp objects got caught in the tornado and then fired back at Drex. They stuck into the side of the barn, pinning Drex to the barn by the sheriff's uniform. Scowling, Drex quickly freed himself.

"Now what?" B-Dawg wondered. "We can't play defense forever!"

Budderball got a determined look in his eye.

"Nobody bullies my brothers and

sis," he said. He dug his right paw into the dirt like a bull and snorted. "Brave like puppy, strong like bull!" Budderball cried.

Drex charged toward Budderball, ready to attack. Budderball used his special power and farted, propelling himself forward like a rocket.

Bam! Budderball hit Drex below the knees. Drex went flying and landed in a crumpled heap. The Buddies cheered.

But Drex wasn't finished yet. He slowly, menacingly rose.

"Enough of this puppy play," he said.

He raised his hands and aimed an electric blast at the tractor. The machine glowed with energy as it rose in the air, floating over the Buddies. Buddha shut his eyes and focused, stopping the tractor in midair.

"I can't hold it forever," Buddha warned. "Mudbud, this is a good time for us to disappear," he instructed.

"Gotcha, dude," Mudbud replied.

Mudbud's collar glowed as he became invisible and then cloaked the rest of the Buddies so they were invisible, too. Buddha held up the tractor just long enough for them to run away, and then the tractor crashed into the ground.

Drex stomped across the farm, looking for the Buddies, as a storm brewed in the sky overhead. A jagged streak of lightning nearly hit him. He quickly dove for cover.

The Buddies ran into the chicken coop to hide, but Drex spotted them just as their camouflage stopped. Drex angrily approached the coop.

B-Dawg was worried. "We're done for, dawgs," he said.

"Super heroes never give up!" Budderball reminded him.

Then they heard Drex, just outside. "I know you're in there. I've run out of time for these silly games. Prepare to be obliterated!"

He raised his hands, getting ready for a big blast. At that moment, a lightning bolt came from the sky. Gramps was standing on the barn roof in his hero costume and planted a lightning rod on the roof. The lightning's energy radiated off the rod and combined with the energy shooting from Drex's fingers. *Zap!* Drex got hit with a double blast.

Inside the coop, the Buddies breathed a sigh of relief.

"It never hurts to have faith, even in your darkest moments," Buddha said.

Mudbud ran for the door. "Dudes, let's go!"

The Buddies ran outside. Billy spotted them through the barn window and called out to them.

"Hey, dawgs, in here, quickly!" he yelled.

The Buddies raced toward the barn. Budderball crashed through the side of the barn, making a hole for the rest of the Buddies to follow him. Drex slowly sat up and spotted them.

"You can't escape me!" he yelled.

He stood up, firing his biggest charge at the doors of the barn.

Boom! The doors exploded into pieces. Drex triumphantly walked in to find the kids and the Buddies standing there. The Buddies were no longer wearing the Rings of Inspiron.

"Give me the rings now, or I will blast you all," he threatened.

Bartleby took a breath and stepped forward. He had the Five Rings of Inspiron in his hand.

"Here they are, Drex, but you have to promise to leave Earth and all of us alone," Bartleby said.

"No, Bartleby, don't!" Alice cried.

"I don't make promises," Drex said. "I make threats. And keep them."

Electricity snaked from his fingers and wrapped around the rings. Then they floated from Bartleby's hands right to Drex.

"That wasn't so hard," he said. "Now that I have the Rings of Inspiron, I will rule this galaxy."

"Just leave us in peace," Sam pleaded.

Drex grinned. "With pleasure. Enjoy your final hour of peace. You see, I've redirected a meteor to collide with Earth. It will land right here in Fernfield."

"No!" Bartleby yelled.

Drex turned to exit the barn just as the real Sheriff Dan walked up, still in Curly's body. Deputy Sniffer stood by his side.

"You there, you are under arrest!" Sheriff Dan said firmly. "Unhand my body this instant!"

Drex shrugged. "If you insist. Please, take it back. It's a sorry bag of charred bones."

Drex's eyes glowed green, and

electricity flowed between him and Sheriff Dan. Drex shape-shifted back into his own body, and Sheriff Dan returned to his body. The pig's eyes grew wide as Curly realized he was back in his own body again. With a squeal, he ran back to the pigpen.

Sheriff Dan hugged and kissed himself. "I love you, body! Oh, how I've missed you so!"

The Buddies and kids left the barn and watched Drex climb into his pod and take off. Monk-E watched from on top of a haystack, glad to see his evil boss go. Gramps climbed down from the roof just as Jack Schaeffer pulled up in his car and jumped out.

"Finally, I found you all," he said.

Bartleby couldn't believe it—his favorite comic book creator was right here, at Fernfield Farms!

"Mr. Schaeffer, sir? Is that really you?" Bartleby asked.

"Yes it is," Jack replied.

Then Bartleby remembered how serious things were. "Drex is gone, but a meteor is heading our way. Drex set its course. Fernfield and the whole planet are doomed!"

They watched as Drex's pod flew up into space. Inside, Drex placed the rings into his power bay.

"All those fools and that disgusting planet will be gone soon, and my future has never been so evil," he said, satisfied.

But his smile faded as he watched the rings melt right in front of his eyes. He realized he had been tricked! But it was too late.

"What's happening? Plastic? My controls . . . they're disabled!"

Drex frantically tried to gain control of the pod, but nothing could be done. His pod was headed right for the meteor.

Boom! The meteor exploded into thousands of pieces.

Earth was saved from the meteor!

CHAPTER 13

Everyone let out a cheer—until Jack looked around, worried.

"Where's Captain Canine?" he asked. Then he spotted the hero lying on the ground by the pigpen.

"Oh no!" Jack cried.

He raced to Captain Canine, picked him up, and carried him back to the others. He gently placed the dog on the grass and knelt beside him. Captain Canine was breathing very faintly.

"Captain Canine was my hero," said Budderball. "I want to be just like him."

Jack nodded. "It was his life's mission to protect the Rings of Inspiron from falling into Drex's evil clutches."

Bartleby pulled the real Rings of Inspiron out of his backpack.

"Well, he accomplished his mission," Bartleby said.

Jack looked surprised. "You mean Drex didn't get the rings?"

"Not exactly," Bartleby replied. "I just wish Captain Canine could have seen this day and taken the rings back to his planet." Bartleby looked sad, but then an excited look crossed his face.

"Wait a second," Bartleby said. He opened his backpack and pulled out an issue of the comic. "'The Rings of Inspiron apart hold great power, but together they have healing power capable of miracles,'" he read out loud. Then he turned to the puppies. "Buddies, surround Captain Canine's body with the rings."

Each Buddy grabbed a ring and they formed a circle around Captain Canine. The rings began to glow. The glow became brighter, forming a circle of energy around the Buddies and Captain Canine. As the others watched, the energy became a tornado of electrically charged blue light.

Finally, it faded. Captain Canine's eyes opened. He slowly sat up.

"Captain Canine! Sir, is that you?" Budderball asked.

Captain Canine looked around. Drex's pod was gone, and the Buddies had the Rings of Inspiron.

"I see you have defeated Drex all on your own," he said. "I knew you could do it. I'm proud of all of you Buddies—you really are super, with or without the rings."

Budderball smiled and said, "We did it together as a team, just like you taught us, Captain Canine. We just had to believe in ourselves."

Relieved, Jack hugged Captain Canine.

"And you, too, Kid Courageous," Captain Canine said.

Billy was surprised. "Wait a minute, dawg. *You're* Kid Courageous?"

Bartleby pulled out a comic that had a photo of Jack on the back. "He writes all of these. It's all real, isn't it, Mr. Schaeffer?"

Jack nodded. "Yes, it is. You think I could make this stuff up? I can't believe it's over and you defeated Drex. How did you do it?"

Bartleby grinned. "We tricked Drex just like Captain Megasis did in issue number one. We gave him the fake rings from the dog food bag."

Jack picked up Bartleby and spun him around.

"You kids and Buddies proved the first rule of being a super hero is . . ."

"You don't have to have super-powers to be a super hero," the kids finished for him.

Suddenly, a bright orange light appeared above the farm.

"Whoa! Look at that!" Bartleby exclaimed, pointing.

A spaceship revealed itself above them. A light beamed down from the ship, and an alien appeared. She was tall, with a large head and big dark eyes. Her skin was pale pink, like her hair. She wore a silvery blue dress, and a silver crown glittered in her hair.

"Greetings, Earthlings," she said in a musical voice. "I am Princess Jorala of Inspiron. As soon as the rings were activated, we started tracking them across the galaxy."

Everyone stared at her in awe. Bartleby stepped forward.

"Hi, I'm Bartleby," he said. "Um . . . welcome to Earth."

"On behalf of all of Inspiron, we thank you for stopping Drex and returning the Rings of Inspiron to the Inspiron people," Princess Jorala said. "Bartleby Livingstone, I heard you were the leader of this victory."

"It was all of us, Your Highness, and especially our Buddies," Bartleby said modestly.

The princess smiled at him and then removed a long necklace from around her neck. The symbol of Inspiron shone on the silver pendant.

"Please accept this as a token of Inspiron's eternal gratitude," she said, placing it over Bartleby's head.

Bartleby couldn't believe it. "Thank you," he said in a thrilled whisper.

"It's always brought me good luck," Princess Jorala said with a wink. Then she looked around the farm. "And where is Captain Megasis?"

Captain Canine stepped forward.

"Here, my princess. I took the form of this dog when I landed on Earth."

"Captain Megasis, you will be a hero on Inspiron. I have missed you so," Princess Jorala said tenderly.

Captain Canine turned to Jack. "Thank you for saving me," he said. "It has been a great pleasure having you as my partner all these years, Jack."

"I couldn't have made it this far without you, my friend," Jack said. "You were like the father to me that I lost."

Jack and Captain Canine hugged.

"Buddies please do the honors and return the Rings of Inspiron to our princess."

B-Dawg whined. "Wait a sec. Do we really have to give the rings back? I was just getting the hang of this super hero stuff. Super B-Dawg!"

"B-Dawg!" Rosebud scolded.

"I was just double-checking," B-Dawg sighed.

The Buddies approached Princess Jorala. She waved her hand and all five rings floated up to her. As the rings glowed, Captain Canine turned back into Captain Megasis, a tall alien with big eyes and pointy ears. He reached out and held Princess Jorala's hand.

"Princess, it's time to go home," he said.

Monk-E slowly walked up to Princess Jorala and bowed. "Excuse me, Your Highness. I am Monk-E, Commander Drex's lieutenant. I would welcome the opportunity to be at your humble service."

Princess Jorala looked at him with her thoughtful eyes for a moment. Finally, she said, "I can see your heart is pure."

Monk-E screeched and climbed onto Megasis's shoulder. Captain Megasis smiled down at the puppies.

"Until we meet again, Buddies."

"Thank you, Captain Megasis," Budderball said.

Mudbud nodded to him. "See you later, alien dude."

119

B-Dawg was as confident as always. "Yo, Captain Megasis, if you ever need a charismatic wing dawg, I'm your Buddy."

A beam of light shot from the spaceship, and Megasis, the princess, and Monk-E began to float back up into the ship. The kids waved good-bye as the ship disappeared into the night sky.

Pete still couldn't believe everything that had happened. "That was epic," he said.

Billy was already imagining the attention he could get. "I can't wait to tell the kids at school."

"You can't tell anyone," Bartleby said. "A super hero must always conceal their true identity to protect the ones they love. We are sworn to secrecy."

The kids took off the Buddies' super hero outfits and stuffed them into Bartleby's backpack—just in time. The news van pulled up to the farm, and the Buddies ran and hid behind the tractor.

Sofia Ramirez and her cameraman dashed out of the news van.

"Kids, what did you see? Is this the work of the Super Pups?" she asked.

"Yes, ma'am!" Bartleby replied, thinking quickly. He needed to come up with a story that would keep the Buddies safe. "The Super Pups saved the day. They left in that spacecraft! They must have been heading home."

Sofia looked confused. "They were aliens?"

"Yeah," Bartleby lied. "They were from another planet. They . . . um . . ."

"Stopped the meteor, and their job here was done," Alice finished for him.

Sofia looked disappointed. She gazed into the camera. "Even though we didn't catch them in action, it is certain that the Super Pups saved the day and the world. We are left with the question, when will the Super Pups return, and where are they now?"

ONE YEAR LATER

A large crowd gathered in Fernfield, eager to hear the announcement. Jack Schaeffer stood at a microphone. Bartleby, in a suit, sat at a table next to him. Behind him were all the Super Buddies in their costumes.

"I know you are all familiar with my last comic book series, *Kid Courageous and Captain Canine*," Jack began, "but we all know that series is over and, I'm happy to say, ended with the happiest of endings. So let me proudly present my new partner in crime, a very talented young man, the brains behind our new operation, Mr. Bartleby Livingstone."

The crowd cheered and Bartleby waved to them. He proudly held up the first issue of a new comic book. He and Jack had created it: *The Adventures of the Super Buddies*!

Budderball wagged his tail and turned to the Buddies.

"Our last adventure might have ended," he said happily, "but it looks like a new one is about to begin!"